Pumpkin
mountain
and
The nightingale

Hannie Truijens

Nelson

Thomas Nelson and Sons Ltd
Nelson House   Mayfield Road
Walton-on-Thames   Surrey
KT12 5PL   UK

51 York Place
Edinburgh
EH1 3JD   UK

Nelson Blackie
Wester Cleddens Road
Bishopbriggs
Glasgow
G64 2NZ   UK

Thomas Nelson (Hong Kong) Ltd
Toppan Building 10/F
22A Westlands Road
Quarry Bay   Hong Kong

Thomas Nelson Australia
102 Dodds Street
South Melbourne
Victoria 3205   Australia

Nelson Canada
1120 Birchmount Road
Scarborough   Ontario
M1K 5G4   Canada

First published by Macmillan Education Ltd 1989

This edition published by Thomas Nelson and Sons Ltd 1992

ISBN 0-17-422498-2
NPN 9 8 7 6 5 4

Printed in China

Pumpkin mountain

Somewhere in China, behind a small village, is a mountain which looks like a giant pumpkin. The people of the village call it Pumpkin mountain.

Long ago there was no mountain behind the village.
The land was flat and divided into small fields.
The poor farmers worked the fields from early in the morning until late in the evening.

In the village lived a poor but cheerful young man.
All he had in the world was the poor little hut which he lived in.
He was a firewood seller and he worked hard all day getting firewood to sell.
He was so tall that he had to bend every time he went in or out of the door of his little hut.
Because he was so tall and poor he was given the nickname Crab.

4

Crab didn't mind being poor.
He sang when he went to get firewood.
At night he played cheerful tunes on his
home-made bamboo flute.

One day Crab came home late from
a hard day's work.
He fell asleep and didn't hear a grey-haired
old man come into the hut.
The old man bent over Crab and said, "I have
brought a magic flute for you. Play on it to
make other people happy."

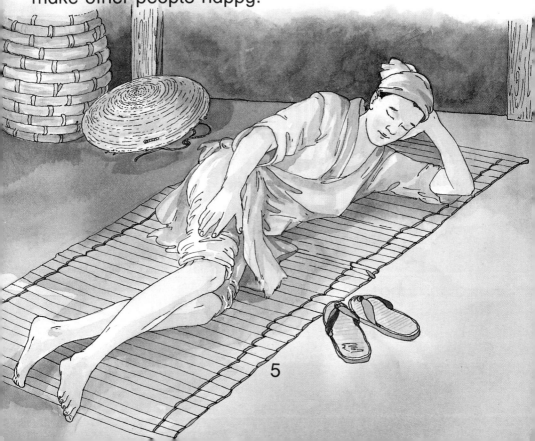

5

Crab woke up.

"It must have been a dream," he said,
but then he saw the bamboo flute.
He put it to his lips and played a tune.
The sound of the flute was so lovely that
Crab played all night long.

From that day on Crab carried the flute
everywhere he went and played to anyone who
would listen.

The music was so cheerful that even the birds
would dance up and down on the branches of
the trees.

One day some children were fishing in the
pond in front of Crab's house.
They caught a small carp and threw it on the
ground. It wriggled and gasped.
   "Put it back in the water before it dies,"
said Crab.
   "We will if you play a tune for us," said
the children.
Crab played a tune and the children put the
carp back into the water.

The next morning Crab was washing himself
with the water of the pond.
A small carp swam up to him.
It was the carp that Crab had saved the
day before.
It was carrying a pumpkin seed in its mouth.
The carp jumped out of the water, put the
pumpkin seed on the land in front of Crab and
dived back into the water.
Crab took the pumpkin seed home and planted
it next to his front door.

A little pumpkin plant came up a
few minutes later and before night the
pumpkin plant had grown so big that it was
already flowering.
It gave only one flower, but in a few days
the flower had turned into a lovely pumpkin.

The pumpkin grew so big and was such a
lovely colour that people came from far and
wide to admire it.

One warm night, when the moon
was full, Crab sat outside.
He had had visitors all day long and
was very tired.
He pulled out his flute and began to play.
He found himself playing tunes that he had
never heard before – magic tunes.
   Suddenly the pumpkin opened up and a
lovely young girl stepped out of it.
And only an empty shell was left of the
lovely big pumpkin.

"I am the pumpkin girl," said the lovely
young girl.
"I want to thank you for looking after
me so well.
Do you want me to stay with you and
be your wife?"
Crab was very happy.
He took the girl by the hand, bowed
to the moon and the earth, and
then they got married.

Crab and the pumpkin girl were very
happy together.
Every evening, when Crab had sold all his
firewood, he went home to find the pumpkin
girl waiting for him.

One day one of the emperor's servants rode
past Crab's hut.
He saw the pumpkin girl and knew that she
must be the most beautiful girl in the world.
He went back to the palace and told the
emperor what he had seen.

The emperor sent two soldiers to the hut
to fetch the pumpkin girl.
Crab begged them not to take his wife, but
they pushed him aside.

His wife said, "Wait patiently and
don't be afraid. Give me the pumpkin shell and
come to visit me at the emperor's
palace in seven days' time."

The impatient soldiers took her by the
arms and dragged her off to the palace.

When the emperor saw the pumpkin girl he fell in love with her.

"Will you stay with me for ever?" he asked.

"Yes, I will," said the pumpkin girl, "but I don't really like this palace."

"Do you know a lovelier palace?" asked the emperor in surprise.

"Yes, I do," said the pumpkin girl. "In the east, seven days journey away from here, is a crystal palace. Only the Son of Heaven can see the crystal palace."

"But I am the Son of Heaven," said
the emperor.

"Then you will be able to see the crystal
palace," said the pumpkin girl.

The emperor started his journey to the
east and took the pumpkin girl with him.

When they had travelled for seven days the
pumpkin girl threw the pumpkin shell into
the ground in front of her.

"Turn into a crystal palace," she whispered.
At once a beautiful crystal palace rose out
of the ground.

The emperor was very happy with the new palace and went inside with his servants.
As soon as they were inside, the palace went back into the ground, with everyone who was in it, and they were never seen again.
In its place rose a high mountain with the shape of a pumpkin.

On the seventh day Crab walked to the emperor's old palace, as his wife had told him to do.
To his surprise, the palace was empty.

Suddenly the pumpkin girl stood before him.
He took her into his arms and stroked her
lovely black hair.

"Would you like to stay in the emperor's
palace?" he asked her.

"No, I would like to go home with you to
our hut in the village," she said.

Crab and the pumpkin girl went back to
their hut and there they lived very long and
very happily.

The nightingale

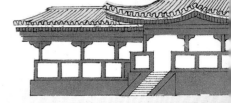

Long, long ago the Chinese emperor lived
in the most beautiful palace in the world.
His garden was also very beautiful.
At the end of the garden was a forest and
in the forest lived a nightingale.

Visitors from other countries praised
the beauty of the palace and the garden but
when they heard the nightingale sing they
said, "That is the most beautiful of all."

18

Some of the visitors wrote books about their travels, and one day such a book came into the hands of the emperor.
He was very pleased with the praise of his palace and garden.
Then he read, "But the nightingale is the most beautiful of all."

"What does that mean?" asked the emperor. "The nightingale? I don't know any nightingale. Is there really such a bird in my garden?" He called his chamberlain.

"Go and find me the nightingale that sings in my garden," ordered the emperor. "The whole world knows what I have in my garden except me."

"I have heard nothing about a nightingale," said the chamberlain, "but I will do my best to find him for you."

The chamberlain asked all the servants in the palace and all the gardeners in the garden, but they could not tell him where the nightingale was to be found.

20

The emperor was angry with the chamberlain and told him to try again. At last the chamberlain found a little kitchen maid who knew the nightingale.

"He lives in a big tree at the very end of the forest," she said.
"Every night I bring my sick mother the left-overs from the kitchen.
On my way home I stop to listen to the nightingale.
I get tears in my eyes when I hear him sing."

"Bring me to this nightingale," said the chamberlain, "and I will reward you."

21

The little kitchen girl took the
chamberlain to the end of the forest where
they found the nightingale.

"Dear little nightingale," she said,
"our emperor would like you to sing for him
tonight. Please come with us."

"It is best to listen to me outside,"
said the nightingale, "but if the emperor
wishes I will sing for him in his palace."

The emperor had a special hall prepared and a golden stand put in the middle of the hall. Everyone put on their best clothes to listen to the nightingale.

The song of the nightingale was so lovely that the emperor had tears in his eyes.

"How can I reward you, little bird?" asked the emperor.

"Your tears are my reward," said the nightingale.

The nightingale was given a golden cage in the palace and every day he was taken out for a walk by twelve servants.

He wasn't very happy in his cage and didn't enjoy his walks with the servants. But every evening he sang for the emperor, and the emperor's tears were his reward.

One day a parcel was delivered to the palace. It came from the emperor of Japan.

24

There was a clockwork nightingale
in the parcel.
It was made of precious metals and jewels and
when the key was wound up it started to sing.
It could only sing one song, which was
not nearly as lovely as the song of the
real nightingale.

The emperor ordered the two nightingales
to sing together, but that sounded horrible.

"It's the fault of the real nightingale,"
said the chamberlain.

25

The clockwork nightingale then had to sing alone.

It was wound up thirty times and thirty times it sang the same song.

It never got tired. Nobody noticed that the real nightingale had flown away.

Everyone praised the clockwork nightingale. They praised its looks and its song.

Soon even the emperor forgot that the song of the real nightingale was much lovelier.

Only the little kitchen maid still listened to the real nightingale.

26

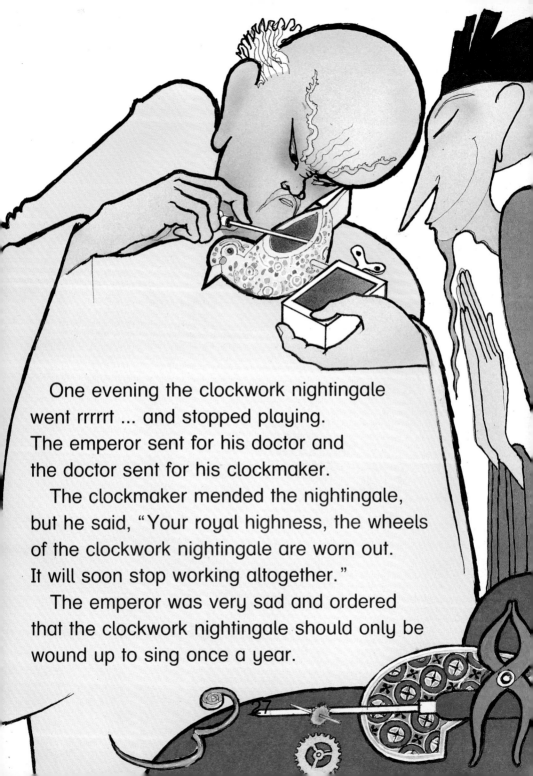

One evening the clockwork nightingale
went rrrrrt ... and stopped playing.
The emperor sent for his doctor and
the doctor sent for his clockmaker.

The clockmaker mended the nightingale,
but he said, "Your royal highness, the wheels
of the clockwork nightingale are worn out.
It will soon stop working altogether."

The emperor was very sad and ordered
that the clockwork nightingale should only be
wound up to sing once a year.

The clockwork nightingale played
once a year for five years.
Then the emperor fell ill, and
no one could find out what was wrong with him.
He became weaker and weaker and it was
clear that he would soon die.

The poor emperor could hardly breathe.
He felt something heavy on his chest.
He opened his eyes and saw Death sitting
on his chest. Death had already put
on the emperor's golden crown.

Death started to list all the bad
things the emperor had done.
The emperor said, "I don't remember," or,
"I didn't know that was bad."
Death went on until the emperor cried out,
"Music, music. Please sing for me, golden bird."
There was no one to wind up the
clockwork nightingale.

Then a beautiful song came through the
window. It was the nightingale.
He had heard that the emperor was
very ill and had come to comfort him.

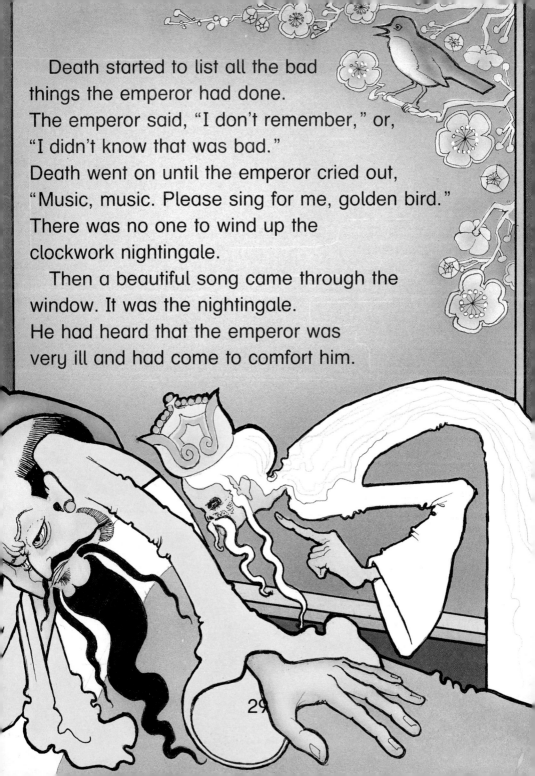

29

At once the emperor started to
feel better.

Death also listened to the
song of the nightingale.
When it stopped, Death said,
"Please keep singing little bird."

"I will sing for you if you give me the
emperor's crown," said the nightingale.

Death gave the crown to the nightingale.
It sang a song about a quiet graveyard.
Death became homesick for his own quiet
garden and drifted out of the window.

"Thank you little nightingale," said the emperor, "you have chased death away from me. Please stay with me. You need only sing when you feel like it and I will break the clockwork nightingale into a million pieces."

"Don't do that." said the nightingale. "It has done what it can. Keep it with you. I cannot live in the palace but I will come and sing for you when I feel like it."

"I will sing to you about happy and
sad people.
I will sing to you about the good and evil
in your empire that is hidden from you.
I fly everywhere and hear everything.
But you must never tell anyone that you have
a little bird who tells you these things."
The nightingale flew away.

The chamberlain came in to cry over
the emperor, as he was sure that the emperor
would be dead by now.

How surprised he was when he heard the
emperor say, "Good morning."

32